HARRAP'S MYSTERIES

THE MYSTERY OF THE HOUND OF BASKERVILLE

d'après

Sir Arthur Conan Doyle

Texte adapté par Anna Culleton d'après le roman
The Hound of the Baskervilles de Sir Arthur Conan Doyle.

Direction de la publication : Carine Girac-Marinier
Rédaction des questions de compréhension : Laurence Bordas
Édition : Sharareh Maljaei, Marie-Noëlle Tilliette
Conception graphique : Sophie Rivoire
Informatique éditoriale : Philippe Cazabet
Mise en page : Tiphaine Desmoulière
Fabrication : Rebecca Dubois

21, rue du Montparnasse
75283 Paris Cedex 06
Harrap's® est une marque de Larousse SAS

ISBN 978 2 81 870745 6

En anglais le temps du récit s'appelle **le prétérit**,
regarde bien comment on le forme :

to be devient **WAS / WERE**

Ensuite, soit les verbes sont réguliers et on leur rajoute **–ED** :

to point → pointed

to seem → seemed

to happen → happened

to follow → followed

Soit ils sont **irréguliers** et tu dois les apprendre !
En voici quelques exemples :

to come → came

to say → said

to hear → heard

to go → went

to fall → fell

to do → did

Tu trouveras les autres dans le vocabulaire !

Pour bien comprendre le début de l'histoire...

Le célèbre détective Sherlock Holmes est sollicité pour intervenir sur une étrange affaire : Sir Charles Baskerville a été retrouvé mort, dans son manoir, près des traces d'un chien gigantesque. Or, d'après une légende médiévale, la famille des Baskerville serait maudite et poursuivie par un chien infernal. Beaucoup de ses membres ont ainsi été frappés de morts subites et mystérieuses. Qui plus est, l'héritier du défunt, Sir Henry, qui doit se rendre dans le Devon pour prendre possession du manoir, a déjà reçu un message de menace lui enjoignant de se tenir écarté de ce lieu.

Dès lors, comment assurer sa sécurité ? Très occupé à Londres, Sherlock Holmes décide d'envoyer son fidèle ami, Watson, à Baskerville, afin de veiller sur Sir Henry. Avant le départ, il prévient Watson : sa mission est très dangereuse et il sera content s'il le revoit vivant…

The characters in the story

Sherlock Holmes

He describes himself as “a specialist in crime”.
He has an international reputation.

Watson

A doctor and great friend of Sherlock Holmes.
He helps Holmes with his investigations.

Henry Baskerville

He is in his thirties. He is the **heir** to Baskerville Hall situated in Devon, England.

Jack Stapleton

He is a naturalist who lives next door to Baskerville Hall.

Mr and Mrs Barrymore

This couple have been servants at Baskerville Hall for many years.
Mr Barrymore is the **butler**. His wife is the cook.

Beryl Stapleton

She lives near Baskerville Hall and is admired for her great beauty.

Selden

An escaped prisoner.

Frankland

He is an **elderly** man with an interest in astronomy. He lives a few kilometres away from Baskerville Hall.

Lestrade

He is one of the best detectives at Scotland Yard. He often works with Holmes.

VOCABULARY

- **thirty** ['θɜ:tɪ] trente
  he is in his thirties il a une trentaine d'années
- a **heir** [eə] un héritier, une héritière
- a **butler** ['bʌtlə] un majordome
- **elderly** ['eldəlɪ] âgé(e)

1 The curse of the Baskervilles

Sherlock Holmes, Dr Watson and Sir Henry Baskerville are at the train station. Watson and Sir Henry are on their way to Baskerville Hall to begin the investigation into the death of Sir Charles Baskerville. Just before they get on the train, Sherlock Holmes says: “Do not go on the **moor** at night”.

“Sir Henry! Why did Holmes say that?” asks Dr Watson.

“To understand, I must tell you about the **curse** of the Baskervilles,” answers Sir Henry. “Sir Hugo Baskerville was a terrible man. One night he kidnapped a young girl and kept her prisoner. But she escaped through the window and **climbed down** the **ivy** on the wall.

Sir Hugo was so furious he promised to give his **soul** to the Powers of **Evil** if he found her again.

He **released** his dogs to **catch** the girl. Then he **rode out** after her **across** the moor.”

VOCABULARY

- the **moor** [mʊə] la lande
- a **curse** [kɜːs] une malédiction
- to **climb down** [ˌklaɪm 'daʊn] descendre
- the **ivy** ['aɪvɪ] le lierre
- a **soul** [səʊl] une âme
- the **Evil** ['iːvl] le Mal
- to **release** [rɪ'liːs] lâcher
- to **catch** [kætʃ] attraper
- to **ride out** [ˌraɪd 'aʊt] poursuivre à cheval
  rode [rəʊd] (passé de **to ride**)
- **across** [ə'krɒs] à travers

What do you understand?

1. **Sherlock Holmes and Doctor Watson go to Baskerville Hall where they meet Sir Henry.**
   - ❑ True, the two detectives arrive in Devon by train.
   - ❑ False, Watson and Sir Henry go to Baskerville Hall by train but Sherlock Holmes doesn't accompany them.

2. **At the train station Sherlock Holmes's instruction to Sir Henry is essential, what does he ask Sir Henry?**
   - ❑ Sir Henry can't go outside Baskerville Hall, it is locked.
   - ❑ Sir Henry can go on the moor alone.
   - ❑ Sir Henry mustn't go on the moor at night.

3. **What did Sir Hugo Baskerville do?**
   - ❑ He locked a young girl and her dog into a room without any light and food.
   - ❑ He kidnapped a young girl and kept her as a prisoner but she escaped.
   - ❑ He kept a young girl as a prisoner with a huge dog in Baskerville Hall.

4. **Complete the sentences with the following words:**

   moor, happened, wall, catch, climbed.

   The young girl __________ down the ivy on the __________, she went to the __________ but Sir Hugo wanted to __________ her with his dogs. He went after her, what __________ next?

What happened to Sir Hugo and the girl?

Choose the best word:

Sir Hugo was very *angry* / *relieved* / *quiet* when she escaped and he promised to give his *castle* / *paintings* / *soul* to the Powers of *Good* / *Evil*.

2 A deadly hound

Sir Henry continues the story: "Sir Hugo's friends were worried and went out to find him. On the way they met a **shepherd** who was very frightened.

'I saw Sir Hugo with the dogs following a girl. There was a monstrous beast **pursuing** them, a **hound** of hell,' said the shepherd.

The men continued their search and shortly after found the poor girl, dead of fear and fatigue. They also discovered Hugo's body beside a great, black beast like a hound. It had **ripped** Hugo's **throat out**.

This **beast** has haunted my family ever since."

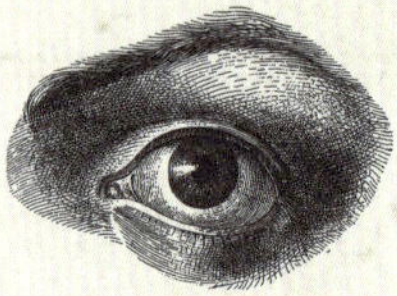

VOCABULARY

- a **shepherd** ['ʃepəd] un berger / une bergère
- to **pursue** [pə'sjuː] poursuivre
- a **hound** [haʊnd] un chien
- to **rip out** [ˌrɪp 'aʊt] déchirer
  ripped [rɪpt] (passé de **to rip**)
- the **throat** [θrəʊt] la gorge
- a **beast** [biːst] une bête

What did the hound do?

1. **Why did Sir Hugo's friends go after him?**

❑ Because he was so furious that they were worried.
❑ Because it was dark outside and he didn't have a light.
❑ Because they feared he might be cold.

2. **Find the missing words!**

On the ________ (= lande), the friends met a ________ (= berger). He saw Sir Hugo following the girl and a monstrous _______ (= chien de chasse) was pursuing them.

3. **The men discovered the girl's body and:**

❑ They found Sir Hugo's body lying next to a beast like a hound.
❑ They found the hound's body next to a rock.
❑ They found Sir Hugo standing beside the hound's body.

4. **How did Sir Hugo die?**

❑ The young girl killed him with the help of her dog.
❑ A black hound ripped his throat out.
❑ He was killed by his monstrous friends.

5. **Choose the best word.**

Sir Henry believes that the beast like a hound still *befriends / haunts / saves* his family.

3 A prisoner has escaped

Watson and Sir Henry **get off** the train at Devonshire station.

A **carriage** is waiting to take them to Baskerville Hall.

On the way, they are very surprised to see a soldier guarding the road.

VOCABULARY

- to **get off** [ˌget 'ɒf] descendre
- a **carriage** ['kærɪdʒ] une calèche
- a **coachman** ['kəʊtʃmən] un cocher
- to **escape** [ɪ'skeɪp] s'évader, s'échapper
  escaped [ɪ'skeɪpt] (passé de **to escape**)
- a **jail** [dʒeɪl] une prison
- **gloomy** ['glu:mɪ] lugubre
- a **butler** ['bʌtlə] un majordome
- a **cook** [kʊk] un cuisinier / une cuisinière

The **coachman** tells them that a prisoner, a murderer, has **escaped** from **jail**. The prisoner's name is Selden.

A little later, the carriage comes to the end of an alley.

A large **gloomy** shape appears over the trees... It is Baskerville Hall.

A man comes out of the shadows to open the door. It is Barrymore, the **butler**. Behind him is his wife, the **cook**.

"Welcome, Sir Henry," says Barrymore.

Who do they see on their way?

Choose the best word.

On their way to Baskerville Hall they are *frightened / pleased / surprised* to see a soldier guarding the *station / road / jail*.

What do they learn at the train station?

1. How did Watson and Sir Henry go to Baskerville Hall from Devonshire station?

- ❑ They went on a carriage that was waiting for them.
- ❑ They went to Baskerville Hall by horse.
- ❑ They went to Baskerville Hall by car.

2. Why is the soldier there?

- ❑ The soldier is searching for the deadly hound after Sir Hugo's death.
- ❑ The soldier, called Selden, is looking for a prisoner who has escaped from jail.
- ❑ The soldier is searching for Selden, a murderer who has escaped from prison.

3. Choose the best word.

We learn some details about the prisoner thanks to the *coachman / butler / cook*.

4. The carriage arrives at the end of an alley. The coachman has taken them to Baskerville Hall. How do we know that the place looks dreadful? Select the correct detail!

- ❑ "Behind him is his wife"
- ❑ "It is Barrymore, the butler"
- ❑ "A large gloomy shape"

4 Watson investigates on the moor

Watson and Sir Henry have dinner.

They are tired after the **journey** and go to bed just after dinner.

VOCABULARY

- a **journey** ['dʒɜːnɪ] un voyage
- to **toss and turn** [tɒs ənd tɜːn] tourner et se retourner
- a **neighbour** ['neɪbə] un voisin / une voisine
- **what is it?** [wɒt ɪz ɪt] qu'est-ce que c'est ?
- the **mire** [maɪə] le bourbier (endroit où la boue est très profonde)
- to **get stuck** [ˌget 'stʌk] s'embourber
  got [gɒt] (passé de **to get**)
- a **butterfly** ['bʌtəflaɪ] un papillon
- to **add** [æd] ajouter

Watson doesn't sleep very well. He **tosses and turns** all night. A deathly silence covers the house. Suddenly he hears a noise. It seems to be a woman crying.

Watson sits up in bed and listens but the crying stops.

The next day, Watson goes for a walk on the moor. He meets a **neighbour**, Jack Stapleton.

Stapleton is a naturalist and passionate about insects. Watson sees something moving in the distance and asks **what it is**.

"It's called Grimpen **Mire**, a dangerous place for men and animals: a pony **got stuck** in there recently and disappeared into the mire," says Stapleton.

"Look at this **butterfly**. Very interesting," he **adds**.

Who does Watson meet on the moor?

Choose the best word.

The next day *Watson / Sir Henry / Holmes* walks on the moor and meets Jack Stapleton who is Baskerville Hall's *butler / neighbour / prisoner*. As a *biologist / naturalist / doctor*, Stapleton is interested in *hounds / horses / insects*.

Why is the moor dangerous?

1. Complete the text with the following words:

journey / noise / sleep / early / dinner.

After __________ at Baskerville Hall the two men go to bed __________ because the __________ was tiring but Doctor Watson doesn't __________ well. Suddenly he can hear a strange __________.

2. Watson thinks he has heard a woman crying but then he can't hear her anymore.

- ❑ True, he listens but the crying stops.
- ❑ False, he sits up in bed and hears a man crying.

3. Why is Grimpen Mire a dangerous place?

- ❑ Because the escaped prisoner is over there.
- ❑ Because people or animals can get stuck into the mire.
- ❑ Because there are lots of butterflies in the sky.

4. Stapleton tells Watson about a pony, what happened to the pony?

- ❑ It went into the mire and was very dirty afterwards.
- ❑ It met the hound in the mire and was killed.
- ❑ It went into the mire and could not escape.

5 Strange things happen

While Stapleton is chasing the butterfly, Watson hears footsteps. He turns around and sees a tall, beautiful woman coming towards him. Watson is **stunned**.

"Go back! Go straight back to London," says the woman.

"Quiet! My brother is coming back," she adds.

"Hello Beryl! Do you know Doctor Watson?" says Stapleton.

"Doctor Watson? You are not Sir Henry?" asks Beryl.

"No I am a friend of his," replies Watson.

The young woman **blushes**. Clearly she thought that Watson was Sir Henry. On his way back to Baskerville, Watson thinks it all seems very strange.

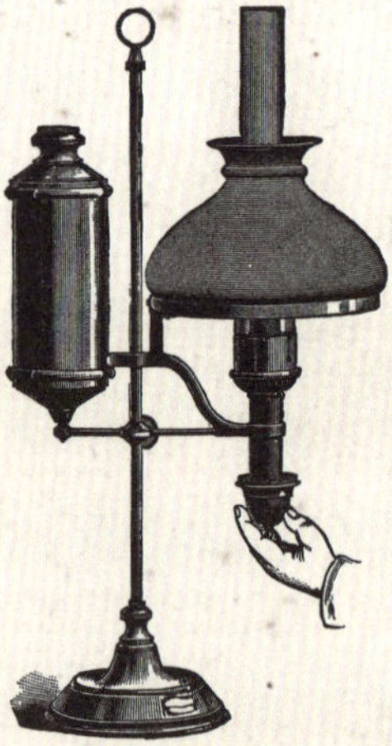

That night Watson once again **wakes up** and hears a sound. This time he hears footsteps in the corridor. The doctor quietly opens his door and sees Barrymore going into a room with a candle in his hand. He looks out the window for a few minutes, then **blows out** the candle and leaves.

The next morning, Watson tells Sir Henry what he saw during the night.

"Decidedly, curious things happen in this house. One of my boots has disappeared. It was **brand new**," says Sir Henry.

VOCABULARY

- to **be stunned** [bi: stʌnd] être abasourdi(e)
- to **blush** [blʌʃ] rougir
- to **wake up** [ˌweik 'ʌp] se réveiller
- to **blow out** [ˌbləʊ 'aʊt] souffler, éteindre
- **brand new** [ˌbrænd 'nju:] tout neuf, toute neuve

What happens at night?

1. **What is the relationship between Beryl and Jack Stapleton?**
   - ❑ Beryl says Jack is her brother.
   - ❑ Beryl says they are married.
   - ❑ Beryl says Jack is her fiancé.

2. **At night Watson can hear someone crying.**
   - ❑ True, Watson can hear a woman crying like the day before.
   - ❑ False, Watson wakes up and he only hears footsteps.

3. **What does Barrymore the butler do at night?**
   - ❑ He leaves a candle by a window in a room and blows his nose as a signal.
   - ❑ He goes into a room, opens a window and waves at someone outside.
   - ❑ He stays with a candle in front of a window and after a few minutes he blows it out as a signal.

4. **When Sir Henry learns about Barrymore's curious activity at night, he adds another curious thing that happened to him, what is it?**
   - ❑ Someone took his collection of butterflies.
   - ❑ Someone took one of his brand new boots.
   - ❑ Someone killed his dog.

6 Love at first sight!

The next day, Sir Henry meets Beryl for the first time. It is **love at first sight**. Soon after, they arrange to meet on the moor. When Watson hears this, he reminds Sir Henry what Holmes said to him about going there.

"Don't worry, Beryl will be with me. I won't be alone," answers Sir Henry.

When Sir Henry and Beryl are out walking, he puts his arms around her and asks her to marry him.

VOCABULARY

- **love** [lʌv] l'amour
  it's love at first sight c'est le coup de foudre
- to **apologise** [ə'pɒlədʒaɪz] s'excuser
- to **call** [kɔ:l] passer, rendre visite
- **protective** [prə'tektɪv] protecteur(trice)
- **used** [ju:st] **to get used to** s'habituer à

"That is impossible, Henry. You must leave this place!" replies Beryl.

Just then, Stapleton appears beside them. He is furious to see that Sir Henry is trying to seduce his sister and he forces Beryl to go home.

That afternoon, Stapleton **calls** to Baskerville Hall to **apologise** to Sir Henry.

He explains that he is very close to his sister and is very **protective** of her.

"Could you keep your feelings from her for three months? That will give me time to **get used to** the idea of separation," asks Stapleton.

"Yes, I'll try," replies Sir Henry.

What does Stapleton do?

Choose the best word.

Jack Stapleton is *furious / frightened / amazed* because Sir Henry and Beryl are falling in love with each other. He tells his sister that she *may / can / must* go back home. He is very *distant / protective / indifferent* of her.

What happens on the moor?

1. **When Sir Henry and Beryl meet the next day they fall in love immediately.**
   - ☐ True, they fall in love the first time they see each other.
   - ☐ False, Beryl tells Sir Henry that he must leave Baskerville Hall.

2. **Watson doesn't want Sir Henry to go on the moor. But Sir Henry isn't worried because:**
   - ☐ He will go with Beryl.
   - ☐ He will take his dogs.
   - ☐ He will ask Watson to come with him.

3. **When Sir Henry and Beryl are on the moor:**
   - ☐ Jack Stapleton asks Sir Henry to marry Beryl because he is in love with her.
   - ☐ Beryl asks Sir Henry to leave the place because she fears Jack's reaction.
   - ☐ Sir Henry asks Beryl if she is married because he is in love with her.

4. **Complete the text with the following words:**

   months / explains / separation / apologise.

   Jack Stapleton calls to __________ to Sir Henry. He __________ that he needs three __________ to get used to the __________ from his sister.

7 Mrs Barrymore's secret

That night, Watson and Sir Henry set a **trap** for Barrymore. They wait for him to appear and then follow him. The **butler** enters the room as before and stands in front of the window holding a **candle**.

"What are you doing here, Barrymore?" asks Watson.

Barrymore jumps, his voice trembling.

"It's not my secret. I cannot tell it," answers Barrymore.

"It's true. It's not his secret, it's mine," says a woman's voice.

VOCABULARY

- a **trap** [træp] un piège
- a **butler** ['bʌtlə] un majordome
- a **candle** ['kændl] une bougie
- **unhappy** [ʌn'hæpɪ] malheureux(euse)
- to **starve** [stɑːv] avoir très faim, mourir de faim
- a **convict** ['kɒnvɪkt] un détenu

The three men turn around to see Mrs Barrymore in the room.

"My **unhappy** brother" explains Mrs Barrymore, "**is starving** out on the moor. The **candle** is a signal to tell him that food is ready."

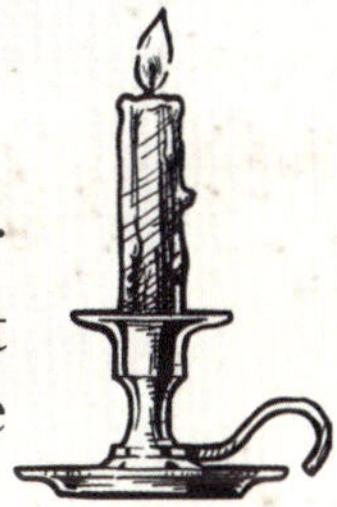

Sir Henry says, "Then your brother is…"

"Selden", she replies, "the escaped **convict**".

At that moment, Watson understands that the cries he hears during the night, are Mrs Barrymore's.

Who is the food for?

Choose the best word.

Mrs Barrymore appears in the room suddenly and explains to Watson and Sir Henry that she has a *candle / trap / secret*: she prepares a basket of *boots / butterflies / food* for her hungry brother and at night her husband shows a candle by the window as a signal to say the food is ready for him.

What is Mrs Barrymore's secret?

1. **Watson and Sir Henry want to understand why Barrymore shows a candle by the window at night. So they decide to follow him and set him a trap.**
   - ❑ True, they wait for him to appear and surprise him.
   - ❑ False, they ask his wife what he is doing at night.

2. **Does Barrymore explain to Watson what he is doing?**
   - ❑ Yes, he tells him his secret.
   - ❑ No, he tells him it's someone else's secret.

3. **"Barrymore jumps, his voice is trembling." What does it show about Barrymore?**
   - ❑ Barrymore is surprised and frightened to see Watson and Sir Henry.
   - ❑ Barrymore is pleased to see Watson and Sir Henry, he needs help.
   - ❑ Barrymore is furious, he wants to keep his secret.

4. **Mrs Barrymore has got a brother! And she is worried about him, that's why she cries at night. Who can it be?**
   - ❑ It is the soldier guarding the road.
   - ❑ It is the escaped prisoner.
   - ❑ It is the coachman.

8 On the moor at night

As soon as the Barrymores leave the room, Sir Henry and Watson decide to **capture** the prisoner. The two men run out across the moor. They soon **spot** the convict. He is running fast and disappears in the distance.

The two men decide to go home. Holmes would be furious if he knew that Sir Henry was on the moor at night. Suddenly they hear a wild **howl**.

"It's a hound!" exclaims Sir Henry. "We often hear this sound on the moor. People here think it's the hound of the Baskervilles!"

Watson and Sir Henry start to run faster and faster. Suddenly, the doctor **notices** the **shadow** of a man on top of the **rocks**. He wants to show Sir Henry but the shadow disappears.

"There was a man on the rocks, I'm sure," says the doctor. "Strange. It was not Selden. He went in the opposite direction. **Perhaps** it was a soldier."

The men go back home, **perplexed**.

VOCABULARY

- to **capture** ['kæptʃə] capturer
- to **spot** [spɒt] apercevoir
- a **howl** [haʊl] un hurlement
- to **notice** ['nəʊtɪs] remarquer
- a **shadow** ['ʃædəʊ] une ombre
- a **rock** [rɒk] un rocher
- **perhaps** [pə'hæps] peut-être
- **perplexed** [pə'plekst] perplexe

What are the two men doing on the moor at night?

I. **Watson wants Sir Henry to go back home because:**

- ❑ Sir Henry must go back to bed.
- ❑ Watson thinks Sir Henry will catch a cold.
- ❑ Holmes doesn't want Sir Henry to go on the moor at night.

2. **The two men can hear a horrible howl. Sir Henry says it is usual to hear this sound and people say it must be the hound of the Baskervilles.**

- ❑ True, they are frightened, they run fast to go back home.
- ❑ False, it must be the escaped prisoner who is lost on the moor.

3. **On their way home Watson spots a shadow on top of the rocks in the distance, what is it?**

- ❑ The shadow of a man
- ❑ The shadow of a big dog
- ❑ The shadow of a pony

4. **The shadow soon dispappears, Watson is not sure about what he saw, he is perplexed.**

- ❑ True, Sir Henry thinks Watson is strange. There is nobody on the moor!
- ❑ False, Watson is sure that he saw a man, he is perplexed because he can't imagine who it is.

Did they catch the prisoner?

Complete the text with the following words:

moor / escapes / convict / capture.

Mrs Barrymore's brother is called Selden, he is an escaped ______ so Watson and Sir Henry want to ______ him. They run out across the ______ but Selden runs faster and he ______ again.

9 A visit to a neighbour

Sir Henry and I heard the strangest ***howling sound*** *on the moor. People here think it is the hound of the Baskervilles. Some even say they have seen it: an enormous beast that is almost phosphorescent.*

Finally, I wanted to tell you that one of Sir Henry's new boots disappeared. Then mysteriously reappeared. But now one of his old boots has disappeared! I'm sure it is nothing but I am reporting the facts as you asked.

Your faithful friend,

Watson

Watson visits Frankland, one of Sir Henry's neighbours, who invited him for a drink. During the conversation, Frankland tells his **guest** that he is an amateur astronomer and that he has a telescope on his **roof**.

He also says he has just **discovered** something very interesting.

"What is it?" says Watson.

"Come with me and you'll see for yourself," replies Frankland.

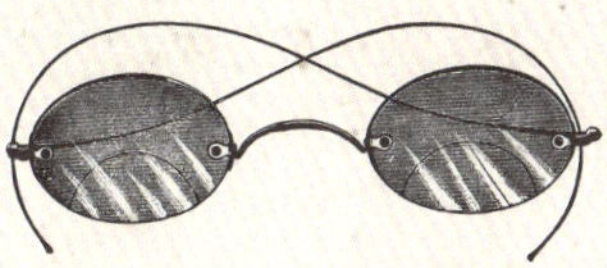

VOCABULARY

- a **howling sound** ['haʊlɪŋ ˌsaʊnd] un hurlement
- a **guest** [gest] un invité / une invitée
- a **roof** [ru:f] un toit
- to **discover** [dɪ'skʌvə] découvrir
  discovered [dɪ'skʌvəd]
  (passé de **to discover**)

Who is the neighbour?

1. **Complete the text with the correct words.**

In a **l**________(6 letters) Watson informs Holmes that they can hear the **h**________ (5 letters) of the Baskervilles howling at **n**________ (5 letters). People describe it as an enormous beast and it is **p**______________ (14 letters): it glows in the dark!

2. **Something mysterious has happened to Sir Henry:**

- ❑ He has lost his two pairs of boots.
- ❑ One of his old boots has disappeared.
- ❑ He can't find one of his brand new boots.

3. **Find the missing words.**

A __________ (= voisin) called Frankland invites Watson for a _________ (= verre). He has discovered something ___________ (= intéressant) and he wants to tell him about it.

4. **Watson meets Sir Henry's neighbour who is fond of:**

- ❑ Butterflies, he is a naturalist.
- ❑ Red wine, he is an amateur oenologist.
- ❑ Watching the stars with his telescope.

5. **Choose the best word.**

An astronomer needs a *telescope/ pair of glasses / glass of wine* to watch the stars.

10 Watson discovers a hut on the moor

Watson is looking through the telescope:

"I see a man… No, a child. He is carrying a bag. He is looking around him as if he doesn't want to be seen," says Watson.

"Exactly! And I know what he's doing! This child is taking **provisions** to the escaped prisoner!" exclaims Frankland.

Watson **pauses** to think. Frankland must be wrong. Barrymore takes food to Selden. This boy is taking provisions to someone else. No doubt the mysterious person on the rocks…

Watson leaves Frankland's house and goes out onto the moor to find the boy. He finds prehistoric **huts**. One of them has a roof. That must be where the mysterious person lives.

Watson goes inside the hut. He sees a flat rock with the boy's bag on it. It **contains** food and a piece of paper. The doctor **picks** it **up** and reads "Watson went to Frankland's". Somebody is **spying on** him. He is very annoyed. He decides to wait for the mysterious person. After a while, he hears someone coming. He takes out his revolver. But he hears a familiar voice.

VOCABULARY

- the **provisions** [prə'vɪʒns] les provisions
- to **pause** [pɔ:z] s'arrêter, faire une pause
- a **hut** [hʌt] une hutte, une cabane
- to **contain** [kən'teɪn] contenir
- to **pick up** [pɪk ʌp] prendre, ramasser
- to **spy on** [spaɪ ɒn] espionner

What does Watson discover?

1. **What does Watson see through Frankland's telescope?**
   - ❑ The escaped prisoner
   - ❑ A child with a bag
   - ❑ A pony stuck in the mire

2. **The boy is looking around him because:**
   - ❑ He doesn't want to be seen.
   - ❑ He is afraid of the hound.
   - ❑ He is looking for Selden.

3. **Frankland explains that the boy is taking food to Selden and Watson agrees.**
   - ❑ True, Watson thinks Frankland is right.
   - ❑ False, it is Selden's brother-in-law who takes him food.

4. **Find the missing words!**

   Watson goes out onto the __________ (= lande), perhaps he will see the boy or the ___________ (= mystérieux) person. He discovers a hut with a _________ (= toit) and inside he finds a piece of _________ (= papier) with a message on it.

5. **Watson must discover who is spying on him, but a voice outside sounds familiar, he knows it!**
   - ❑ True, he understands that the boy has spied on him for a mysterious and familiar person.
   - ❑ False, Watson is annoyed because he thinks Selden is the mysterious person.

11 What a surprise!

"Lovely evening, my dear Watson! " says a familiar voice.

Watson **rushes out** of the hut. It is Sherlock Holmes! Happy and surprised, the doctor asks:

"So you are living in this hut! Why?"

"I am hiding from our enemies. Thank you for your letters. I read them very **carefully** and they have helped me see the light," answers Holmes.

VOCABULARY

- to **rush out** [ˌrʌʃ ˈaʊt] sortir précipitemment
- **carefully** [ˈkeəflɪ] attentivement
- a **motive** [ˈməʊtɪv] un mobile
- to **tempt** [tempt] attirer

"So do you know what's happening?" asks Watson.

"Yes but I don't know Stapleton's **motive** yet," replies Holmes.

"Stapleton! But he and his sister..." says Watson.

Holmes explains that Beryl is not Stapleton's sister but his wife. Stapleton used his wife's beauty to **tempt** Sir Henry onto the moor. Sir Henry is in great danger.

What did Stapleton ask Beryl?

Complete the text with the following words:

danger / disappear / because / clues / wife / understand.

Jack Stapleton asked his ________ to tempt Sir Henry onto the moor ________ Jack knows that Sir Henry will be in ________ on the moor. Moreover he wants Sir Henry to ________ but Holmes doesn't ________ his motive, some ________ are still missing.

Who is living in the hut?

I. **The mysterious person happens to be Sherlock Holmes so Watson is:**

❑ Very pleased to see him.
❑ Very cross because his friend is spying on him.
❑ Frightened.

2. **"So you are living in this hut!" means that:**

❑ Holmes has moved to a new house on the moor.
❑ Holmes is staying there for a few days.
❑ Holmes prefers living in a hut.

3. **Talking about Watson's letters Holmes says: "They have helped me see the light", it means:**

❑ The hut is very dark, it is not possible to read inside.
❑ It is dark because it takes place in the evening, Holmes can't read the letters.
❑ Holmes understood the situation thanks to Watson's letters.

4. **Holmes tells Watson that the Stapletons are not brother and sister but a couple!**

❑ True, Jack Stapleton isn't Beryl's brother but her husband.
❑ False, Beryl is Jack's sister.

12 The hound attacks

Suddenly they hear a terrible **scream** coming from the moor.

Holmes **jumps** to his feet. They hear another scream mixed with a sinister bark.

The two men run as fast as they can into the dark night.

"The hound. Come Watson, before it's too late!" exclaims Holmes.

They hear a sound to their left.

At the bottom of a **hill**, they see something dark on the ground.

When they get closer they realise that it is a man.

There is **blood** everywhere. It seems the man was running to escape the hound and fell to his **death**.

Holmes lights a **match**. The **crushed skull** is covered in blood.

The body is wearing a tweed suit: it is Sir Henry!

The two men are horrified and feel **guilty**. They **weren't able to** protect their friend. Then in the **moonlight** Holmes starts to laugh.

"Are you **mad**?" asks Watson.

VOCABULARY

- a **scream** [skri:m] un hurlement
- to **jump** [dʒʌmp] bondir
- a **hill** [hɪl] une colline
- **blood** [blʌd] le sang
- **death** [deθ] la mort
- a **match** [mætʃ] une allumette
- **crushed** [krʌʃt] fracassé(e)
- the **skull** [skʌl] le crâne
- **guilty** ['gɪltɪ] coupable
- to **be able to** [bi: 'eɪbl tu:] pouvoir
  they weren't able to ils n'ont pas pu
- the **moonlight** ['mu:nlaɪt] le clair de lune
- **mad** [mæd] fou, folle

What happened on the moor?

1. **Suddenly Holmes and Watson hear someone screaming and a sinister bark coming from the moor. What is a "bark"?**
   - ❑ A sort of boat
   - ❑ The sound of a dog
   - ❑ The lack of light

2. **The detectives' reaction is to run as fast as they can because they are afraid someone may be killed by the hound.**
   - ❑ True, Holmes says: "Come Watson, before it's too late!"
   - ❑ False, they can't run fast because it is too dark.

3. **As they try to identify the victim with the help of a match, they recognise Sir Henry's tweed suit! They feel guilty because:**
   - ❑ They weren't able to avoid Sir Henry's death.
   - ❑ They succeeded in protecting their friend.
   - ❑ His skull is covered in blood and his suit is dirty too.

4. **Holmes starts doing something strange, Watson thinks he is mad, what does Holmes do?**
   - ❑ He starts a fire to divert wild animals.
   - ❑ He starts crying because he is horrified.
   - ❑ He starts laughing because he notices another clue.

How did the man die?

Can you find the missing words?

On their left, at the **b**__________ of a hill they can see a **d**__________ shape on the ground, they are sure it is a man and they notice **b**__________ all around. The man probably tried to **e**__________ the hound but he **f**__________ down and died.

13 The wrong victim

"A **beard**! This man has a beard! It is not Sir Henry! It is the escaped prisoner," exclaims Holmes.

The men look at the body. It is Selden.

Sir Henry gave some of his old clothes to Barrymore.

Barrymore gave them to Selden, his **brother-in-law**.

"You see, Watson", explains Holmes, "Selden is dead because of the clothes. Stapleton gave the hound Sir Henry's **scent**, from the missing boot. The hound followed the **trail** and found Sir Henry's suit but on Selden".

"But why is the hound out tonight? Is Sir Henry on the moor tonight?" asks Watson.

"We will know in a few seconds", answers Holmes.

"Watson, not a word!" he adds.

VOCABULARY

- a **beard** [bɪəd] une barbe
- a **brother-in-law** ['brʌðəʳ ɪn lɔ:] un beau-frère
- a **scent** [sent] une odeur
- a **trail** [treɪl] une piste

Who is the wrong victim?

1. **Holmes is feeling relieved to see that the man is not Sir Henry! How does he deduce it?**
   - ❑ Because Sir Henry is at Baskerville Hall, he mustn't go on the moor at night.
   - ❑ Because the body has got a beard so it can't be Sir Henry.
   - ❑ Because the moonlight helps him to see the body's face, it is an old man.

2. **The detectives recognise the dead body:**
   - ❑ It is Barrymore, the butler.
   - ❑ It is Sir Henry: Barrymore's brother-in-law.
   - ❑ It is Selden, the escaped prisoner.

3. **Selden died because he was wearing a beard.**
   - ❑ True, the hound followed his trail because he can't bear people with beards.
   - ❑ False, he died because he was wearing Sir Henry's suit.

4. **Choose the best word.**

The two detectives worry about *Stapleton / the prisoner / Sir Henry*. Why is *the hound / Barrymore / the soldier* on the moor tonight?

Why did the hound follow Selden?

Complete the text with the following words:

clothes / brother-in-law / trail / scent / boot.

Selden received Sir Henry's suit from his ____________: Barrymore. Stapleton gave the dog Sir Henry's old ____________ to recognise his ____________. Then the hound went onto the moor and followed Sir Henry's ____________ but pursued Selden instead of Sir Henry because of the ____________!

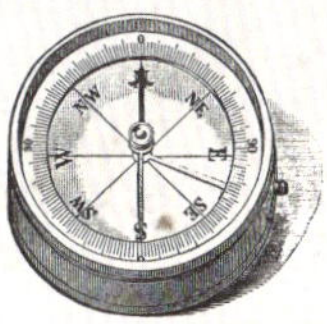

14 Stapleton's disappointment

A man approaches the two friends. It is Stapleton.

"Watson!" he says, "What is it? Is that man **hurt**? Tell me it is not our friend Sir Henry!"

"It's Selden, the prisoner," answers Watson.

They can see the **disappointment** on Stapleton's face.

"I heard a scream. That's why I came out. I was **worried** about Sir Henry. Beryl and I invited him to our house this evening. What a tragedy, Mr Holmes!" explains Stapleton.

"Yes. But how did you recognise me?" asks Holmes.

"You are very famous! We are very **proud** to have you here in Devon," replies Stapleton.

"Alas, not for much longer. I am going back to London tomorrow," says Holmes.

"What a pity! I am sorry but it is late. I must go home to Beryl. Good evening," answers Stapleton.

VOCABULARY

- **hurt** [hɜːt] blessé(e)
- a **disappointment** [ˌdɪsəˈpɔɪntmənt] une déception
- **worried** [ˈwʌrɪd] inquiet(ète)
- **proud** [praʊd] fier(ère)

What is Stapleton doing on the moor?

1. Who suddenly joins the detectives?

❑ Beryl's husband
❑ Barrymore's brother-in-law
❑ The prisoner's sister

2. Where was Stapleton when the tragedy happened?

❑ He was at home with Beryl waiting for Sir Henry, they invited him for dinner.
❑ He was on the moor on his way to Baskerville Hall to fetch Sir Henry.
❑ He was cooking dinner with Beryl at home.

3. While speaking to Stapleton, Holmes announces his plans for the following day:

❑ He is going back to his hut on the moor.
❑ He is leaving because his investigation is over.
❑ He is going back home to London without giving any reason.

4. Complete the text with the correct verbs:

suggests / hopes / learns / notices / wants.

Jack Stapleton __________ Sir Henry is dead so he __________ to check the victim's name. He ____________ Sir Henry's name but when he ___________ the victim is Selden, Watson ________ his disappointment.

15 Portrait of an ancestor

Watson and Holmes go back to Baskerville Hall.

"Why didn't we arrest Stapleton immediately?" says Watson.

"It is too early. I need more **proof**. Don't say anything about the **howls** to Sir Henry. It will make him too nervous for tomorrow," replies Holmes.

"Tomorrow? What is happening tomorrow?" asks Watson. "**As usual** you never tell me your plans!"

"I like to surprise you, Watson", smiles Holmes.

VOCABULARY

- a **proof** [pru:f] une preuve
- a **howl** [haʊl] un hurlement
- **as usual** [ˌæz ˈju:ʒəl] comme d'habitude
- to **stare** [steə] regarder fixement

Sir Henry is very happy to see Sherlock Holmes again.

He explains he didn't go to dinner at the Stapletons' last night as he didn't want to be alone on the moor.

As he speaks, Holmes is **staring** at a painting.

"Who is the man in the portrait? One of your ancestors?" asks Holmes.

"Yes, but not just any ancestor: that is the terrible Hugo of Baskerville!" replies Sir Henry.

Holmes seems very interested.

What are Holmes's plans?

Choose the best word.

Holmes has got *plans / deduction / conclusion* for Sir Henry on the *next / last / previous* day. Sir Henry mustn't be too *angry / nervous / interested* so he doesn't need to know about the howls on the moor. Watson knows *something / anything / nothing* about Holmes's intentions!

Is Stapleton guilty?

1. **Holmes and Watson go back to Sir Henry's place to make sure he is at home. Watson asks Holmes:**
   - ❑ Why don't we arrest Stapleton as you think he is guilty?
   - ❑ Why don't we say anything to Sir Henry about the howls?
   - ❑ Why don't we ask Beryl if she has any useful information?

2. **Holmes doesn't have enough proof to send Stapleton to prison.**
   - ❑ True, he needs more proof.
   - ❑ False, he will call the police to arrest him.

3. **Sir Henry listened to Holmes's advice, he was invited for dinner at the Stapletons' but he didn't go so as not to walk alone on the moor at night.**
   - ❑ True, as Holmes and Watson were not there he didn't want to go out alone.
   - ❑ False, he didn't go because he learned that the Stapletons were married.

4. **During the dinner Holmes seems very interested in the painting on the wall, it shows the portrait of:**
   - ❑ Sir Henry's ancestor called Charles
   - ❑ Sir Hugo of Baskerville
   - ❑ Sir Henry himself

16 Stapleton's motive becomes clear

When Sir Henry goes to bed, Holmes asks Watson to come with him and have a look at the portrait:

"Does the portrait **remind** you of anyone?" asks Holmes.

"The mouth is like Sir Henry's… oh my God! Stapleton!" replies Watson.

"Exactly", exclaims Holmes. "Stapleton is a Baskerville!"

And so Stapleton's motive is clear. He too is an **heir** to Baskerville Hall.

VOCABULARY

- to **remind** [rɪ'maɪnd] rappeler
- a **heir** [eə] un héritier / une héritière
- to **agree** [ə'gri:] accepter
- **on foot** [ɒn fʊt] à pied

The next morning, Holmes tells Sir Henry to do everything he asks without question. Sir Henry **agrees**. Holmes also says that he and Watson will return to London that afternoon.

"Also", adds Holmes, "Stapleton will invite you to dinner again tonight. Accept the invitation and say that after dinner you will go home alone, **on foot**, across the moor".

"Alone, at night, across the moor?" asks Sir Henry, very surprised.

"Very well, I will do it," he adds.

Holmes's instructions

Find the missing words!

Holmes guesses that Stapleton will **i**______ (6 letters) Sir Henry to dinner again that's why the **d**______ (10 letters) are going away from Baskerville Hall, but isn't it **s**______ (10 letters) for Sir Henry to walk **a**______ (5 letters) across the moor at night?

What do you understand about Stapleton's motive?

1. Holmes draws Watson's attention to the portrait and suddenly Watson understands the situation:
   - ❑ Sir Henry is not a Baskerville, his mouth is different.
   - ❑ The portrait reminds them of Selden.
   - ❑ Stapleton looks like Sir Hugo who must be his ancestor too.

2. It means that:
   - ❑ Stapleton wants Sir Henry to disappear so that he could inherit Baskerville Hall.
   - ❑ Sir Henry is not an heir to Baskerville Hall, Stapleton is the only heir.
   - ❑ Stapleton would like to share Baskerville Hall with Sir Henry.

3. In his new plan Holmes will return to London with Watson in the afternoon while Sir Henry is supposed to accept Stapleton's invitation for lunch.
   - ❑ True, the detectives are going back to London leaving Sir Henry alone.
   - ❑ False, Holmes thinks that Stapleton will invite Sir Henry to dinner.

4. Sir Henry doesn't want to listen to Sherlock Holmes because Holmes's plan is too dangerous.
   - ❑ True, he doesn't accept to go across the moor alone at night.
   - ❑ False, he will do everything without question.

17 Holmes sets a trap

In the afternoon, Barrymore drives Holmes and Watson to the station, then leaves. Holmes tells Watson that they will not take the train. It is just a **trick**. Stapleton will feel free to act and they'll be able to catch him.

At the station, Holmes and Watson **meet** Lestrade.

"Ah, here is Lestrade! One of the best detectives at **Scotland Yard**. He will determine the facts," says Holmes.

VOCABULARY

- a **trick** [trɪk] une ruse
- to **meet** [miːt] rencontrer, retrouver
- **Scotland Yard** ancien nom du siège de la police à Londres (aujourd'hui **New Scotland Yard**).
- a **coachman** ['kəʊtʃmən] un cocher

Two hours later, Holmes, Watson and Lestrade go to Stapleton's house. Just before they arrive, they ask the **coachman** to stop.

Then they go on foot, quietly. As soon as they arrive near the house, Watson looks in through the sitting room window. Then he comes back to the others.

"Sir Henry and Stapleton are drinking coffee and smoking cigars. Beryl isn't there," says Watson.

"If they're drinking coffee, dinner is finished. Sir Henry will leave soon," replies Holmes.

What is going on in Stapleton's house?

1. **At the train station Barrymore goes back to Baskerville Hall without waiting for the detectives' train.**
   - ❑ True, so he doesn't notice that they don't take the train to London.
   - ❑ False, he waves them goodbye on the platform.

2. **Who is the person they meet at the train station?**
   - ❑ Lestrade, a new butler for Baskerville Hall
   - ❑ Lestrade, a very clever detective from Scotland Yard
   - ❑ Lestrade, a Scottish policeman invited at Baskerville Hall

3. **Through the window of Stapleton's house, Watson can see the Stapletons and Sir Henry smoking and drinking coffee.**
   - ❑ True, they have just finished their meal.
   - ❑ False, Beryl is not there.

4. **From what they can see through the window they conclude that Sir Henry is about to go back home walking across the moor.**
   - ❑ True, so we can imagine that the detectives will take care of him when he is on the moor.
   - ❑ False, Lestrade thinks that Beryl will accompany Sir Henry to Baskerville Hall.

What is the trick?

Complete the text with the following words:
intervene / trick / think / plan / catch / help.

Holmes's ______ is simple: Stapleton must ______ that Sir Henry is alone at Baskerville Hall. In this way, Stapleton will not fear that Holmes can ______ to defend his friend. Holmes is playing a ______ on Stapleton to ______ him with Lestrade's ______.

18 The hound attacks Sir Henry

Holmes pulls out his revolver.

Watson and Lestrade take out their **weapons**.

They hear footsteps. The three men try to see what is coming out of the dark.

Suddenly a monster from hell jumps out of the **fog**.

It's an enormous black hound **spitting** flames.

It runs towards Sir Henry.

Watson and Holmes are so **stunned** that they don't react.

Then they both shoot at the same time. The beast howls horribly.

It is hurt. But it doesn't stop. Sir Henry turns around, horrified.

The beast jumps on its victim, throws him on the ground and takes his **throat** in its teeth. At the same time, Holmes, running as fast as he can, shoots the animal. The beast **howls** and falls. It is dead.

VOCABULARY

- a **weapon** ['wepən] une arme
- the **fog** [fɒg] le brouillard
- **spitting** ['spɪtɪŋ] crachant
- to **be stunned** [ˌbiː 'stʌnd] être abasourdi(e)
- the **throat** [θrəʊt] la gorge
- to **howl** [haʊl] hurler

Why is Sir Henry in great danger?

1. Which detail shows us that there is no moonlight?

❑ The detectives can hardly see in the distance because it is foggy.

❑ Holmes needs his revolver to see in the dark.

❑ A monster is coming from hell.

2. Why do the detectives need weapons on the moor?

❑ Because the situation is quite safe.

❑ Because they need to defend themselves from the escaped prisoner.

❑ Because Sir Henry is in great danger.

3. What is Sir Henry's reaction when he hears the shooting and the howling?

❑ He throws himself on the ground.

❑ He turns round and is horrified to see the hound after him.

❑ He turns round and shoots at the terrifying hound.

4. Find the missing words.

Suddenly an **e**__________ (= énorme) and dreadful hound is running after Sir Henry. Holmes and Watson **s**_______ (= tirer) at the beast but they only **h**______ (= blesser) it, it howls horribly but it still runs and **j**_______ (= sauter) on its victim.

19 The death of the hound

Sir Henry doesn't move. Holmes **grabs** his shirt. He was not **bitten**. He just **fainted**. A few minutes later, he opens his eyes.

"My God! Where is the beast?" asks Sir Henry.

"It is dead," replies Holmes.

Watson puts his hand on the hound's **muzzle**.

When he takes his hand away, his fingers are **glowing**. **It is phosphorous**! Stapleton put it on his dog to make it glow.

The three men leave Sir Henry to **rest** and go to find the criminal.

But Stapleton is not at home. He ran when he heard the shots. Holmes and his two friends look everywhere in the house.

Upstairs, they find a **locked** door. They kick the door open. Inside they find Beryl, **tied** to a **post**. They free her.

"Sir Henry? Is he safe?" asks Beryl.

"Yes. And the hound is dead," answers Holmes.

Beryl **sighs** with **relief**.

VOCABULARY

- to **grab** [græb] saisir
- to **bite** [baɪt] mordre
  bitten ['bɪtn] (passé de **to bite**)
- to **faint** [feɪnt] s'évanouir
  fainted ['feɪntɪd] (passé de **to faint**)
- the **muzzle** ['mʌzl] le museau
- **glowing** ['gləʊɪŋ] brillant(e), phosphorescent(e)
- **phosphorous** ['fɒsfərəs]
  it's phosphorous c'est du phosphore
  the dog is phosphorous
  le chien est phosphorescent
- to **rest** [rest] se reposer
- **upstairs** [ˌʌp'steəz] à l'étage
- **locked** [lɒkt] fermé(e) à clé
- **tied** [taɪd] attaché(e)
- a **post** [pəʊst] un poteau
- to **sigh** [saɪ] soupirer
- **relief** [rɪ'li:f] soulagement

Let's investigate!

1. **What happened to Sir Henry?**
   - ❑ The hound took his throat in its teeth and killed him.
   - ❑ He fainted and fell on the ground unconscious.
   - ❑ He bit the hound and killed it.

2. **Why was the dog phosphorous?**
   - ❑ Because Stapleton put something glowing on his dog.
   - ❑ Because of the moonlight.
   - ❑ Because it had supernatural powers.

3. **Complete the text with the following words:**

   tied / dead / instead / locked / now / safe.

   _________ that the hound is _________ and Sir Henry is _________, the three detectives go to find Stapleton but he is not at home. _________ they find Beryl _______ in a room and _______ up to a post because she disagreed with her husband.

4. **Stapleton escaped when he heard the shots.**
   - ❑ True, the detectives can't find him at home.
   - ❑ False, he is smoking a cigar at home.

5. **Find the missing words!**

   We know that Beryl doesn't _________ (= partager) her husband's opinion about Sir Henry because she sighs with ___________ (= soulagement) when she learns that Sir Henry is not _________ (= mort).

20 The missing boot

The next day Beryl and the three men go to Grimpen Mire.

There is an island in the middle where Stapleton kept his dog.

Holmes sees a boot in the grass. It is Sir Henry's missing boot.

"Stapleton came here last night. But it was dark and **foggy**. Go and look for **footprints**," says Holmes.

VOCABULARY

- **foggy** ['fɒgɪ] brumeux(euse)
- a **footprint** ['fʊtprɪnt] une empreinte
- to **conclude** [kən'klu:d] conclure
- **while** [waɪl] pendant que
  for a while pendant un certain temps
- to **solve** [sɒlv] résoudre
- to **be bored with** [bi: 'bɔ:d wɪð] s'ennuyer

But they find nothing on the island. Holmes **concludes** that Stapleton's body has disappeared into the mire.

A few days later, Holmes tells Watson that Sir Henry has decided to travel **for a while** to clear his head.

"But that's enough about the Baskervilles. My dear Watson, I have a new mystery to **solve**. Shall I tell you about it?" asks Holmes.

"Oh yes, please," replies Watson.

Watson knows he will never **be bored with** Sherlock Holmes.

Why did Stapleton go to Grimpen Mire?

Choose the best word.

After the dinner with Sir Henry, Stapleton heard the *mystery / shots / bell* and decided to escape; he went to Grimpen Mire but it was foggy and too *rainy / bright / dark* to see, so Holmes explains that he got stuck into the *mire / grass / hut* and probably died there.

What do you understand about the missing boot?

1. **Where did Stapleton keep his dog?**
   - ❑ In the grass in Grimpen Mire.
   - ❑ Next to Grimpen Mire on the moor.
   - ❑ On a small island in Grimpen Mire.

2. **Does Beryl cooperate to help the detectives find her husband?**
   - ❑ Yes, she shows them the place where he kept his dog.
   - ❑ No, she wishes to protect her husband.

3. **Now it is sure that Stapleton organised a plot against Sir Henry to get rid of him. What clue do they find?**
   - ❑ They find Stapleton's shoes on the island, he was wearing Sir Henry's boots instead.
   - ❑ There are Stapleton's footprints everywhere on the moor, he got lost because of the fog.
   - ❑ Holmes notices Sir Henry's missing boot, Stapleton used it for Sir Henry's smell.

4. **Finally Sir Henry is safe but he had a horrible experience so he decides to travel in order to "clear his head", what does it mean?**
   - ❑ He needs a shampoo because his hair is phosphorous like the dog.
   - ❑ He needs to rest and get away from Baskerville Hall.
   - ❑ He needs to solve a new mystery with Sherlock Holmes.

1

1. False, Watson and Sir Henry go to Baskerville Hall by train but Sherlock Holmes doesn't accompany them.

2. Sir Henry mustn't go on the moor at night.

3. He kidnapped a young girl and kept her as a prisoner but she escaped.

4. The young girl climbed down the ivy on the wall, she went to the moor but Sir Hugo wanted to catch her with his dogs. He went after her, what happened next?

What happened to Sir Hugo and the girl?

Sir Hugo was very angry when she escaped and he promised to give his soul to the Powers of Evil.

2

1. Because he was so furious that they were worried.

2. On the moor, the friends met a shepherd. He saw Sir Hugo following the girl and a monstrous hound was pursuing them.

3. They found Sir Hugo's body lying next to a beast like a hound.

4. A black hound ripped his throat out.

5. Sir Henry believes that the beast like a hound still haunts his family.

3

Who do they see on their way?

On their way to Baskerville Hall they are surprised to see a soldier guarding the road.

1. They went on a carriage that was waiting for them.

2. The soldier is searching for Selden, a murderer who has escaped from prison.

3. We learn some details about the prisoner thanks to the **coachman**.

4. "A large gloomy shape".

4

Who does Watson meet on the moor?

The next day **Watson** walks on the moor and meets Jack Stapleton who is Baskerville Hall's **neighbour**. As a **naturalist**, Stapleton is interested in **insects**.

1. After **dinner** at Baskerville Hall the two men go to bed **early** because the **journey** was tiring but Doctor Watson doesn't **sleep** well. Suddenly he can hear a strange **noise**.

2. True, he listens but the crying stops.

3. Because people or animals can get stuck into the mire.

4 It went into the mire and could not escape.

5

1. Beryl says Jack is her brother.

2. False, Watson wakes up and he only hears footsteps.

3. He stays with a candle in front of a window and after a few minutes he blows it out as a signal.

4. Someone took one of his brand new boots.

6

What does Stapleton do?

Jack Stapleton is furious because Sir Henry and Beryl are falling in love with each other. He tells his sister that she must go back home. He is very protective of her.

1. True, they fall in love the first time they see each other.
2. He will go with Beryl.
3. Beryl asks Sir Henry to leave the place because she fears Jack's reaction.
4. Later on Jack Stapleton calls to apologise to Sir Henry. He explains that he needs three months to get used to the separation from his sister.

7

Who is the food for?

Mrs Barrymore appears in the room suddenly and explains to Watson and Sir Henry that she has a secret: she prepares a basket of food for her hungry brother and at night her husband shows a candle by the window as a signal to say the food is ready for him.

1. True, they wait for him to appear and surprise him.
2. No, he tells him it's someone else's secret.
3. Barrymore is surprised and frightened to see Watson and Sir Henry.
4. It is the escaped prisoner.

8

1. Holmes doesn't want Sir Henry to go on the moor at night.

2. True, they are frightened, they run fast to go back home.

3. The shadow of a man.

4. False, Watson is sure that he saw a man, he is perplexed because he can't imagine who it is.

Did they catch the prisoner?

Mrs Barrymore's brother is called Selden, he is an escaped convict so Watson and Sir Henry want to capture him. They run out across the moor but Selden runs faster and he escapes again.

9

1. In a letter Watson informs Holmes that they can hear the hound of the Baskervilles howling at night. People describe it as an enormous beast and it is phosphorescent: it glows in the dark!

2. One of his old boots has disappeared.

3. A neighbour called Frankland invites Watson for a drink. He has discovered something interesting and he wants to tell him about it.

4. Watching the stars with his telescope.

5. An astronomer needs a telescope to watch the stars.

10

1. A child with a bag.

2. He doesn't want to be seen.

3. False, it is Selden's brother-in-law who takes him food.

4. Watson goes out onto the moor, perhaps he will see the boy or the mysterious person. He discovers a hut with a roof and inside he finds a piece of paper with a message on it.

5. True, he understands that the boy has spied on him for a mysterious and familiar person.

11

What did Stapleton ask Beryl?

Jack Stapleton asked his wife to tempt Sir Henry onto the moor because Jack knows that Sir Henry will be in danger on the moor. Moreover he wants Sir Henry to disappear but Holmes doesn't understand his motive, some clues are still missing.

1. Very pleased to see him.
2. Holmes is staying there for a few days.
3. Holmes understood the situation thanks to Watson's letters.
4. True, Jack Stapleton isn't Beryl's brother but her husband.

12

1. The sound of a dog.
2. True, Holmes says: "Come Watson, before it's too late!"
3. They weren't able to avoid Sir Henry's death.
4. He starts laughing because he notices another clue.

How did the man die?

On their left, at the bottom of a hill they can see a dark shape on the ground, they are sure it is a man and they notice blood all around. The man probably tried to escape the hound but he fell down and died.

13

1. Because the body has got a beard so it can't be Sir Henry.
2. It is Selden, the escaped prisoner.

3. False, he died because he was wearing Sir Henry's suit.

4. The two detectives worry about Sir Henry. Why is the hound on the moor tonight?

Why did the hound follow Selden?

Selden received Sir Henry's suit from his brother-in-law: Barrymore. Stapleton gave the dog Sir Henry's old boot to recognise his scent. Then the hound went onto the moor and followed Sir Henry's trail but pursued Selden instead of Sir Henry because of the clothes!

14

1. Beryl's husband.

2. He was at home with Beryl waiting for Sir Henry, they invited him for dinner.

3. He is going back home to London without giving any reason.

4. Jack Stapleton hopes Sir Henry is dead so he wants to check the victim's name. He suggests Sir Henry's name but when he learns the victim is Selden, Watson notices his disappointment.

15

What are Holmes's plans?

Holmes has got plans for Sir Henry on the next day. Sir Henry mustn't be too nervous so he doesn't need to know about the howls on the moor. Watson knows nothing about Holmes's intentions!

1. Why don't we arrest Stapleton as you think he is guilty?

2. True, he needs more proof.

3. True, as Holmes and Watson were not there he didn't want to go out alone.

4. Sir Hugo of Baskerville.

16

Holmes's instructions

Holmes guesses that Stapleton will **invite** Sir Henry to dinner again that's why the **detectives** are going away from Baskerville Hall but isn't it **surprising** for Sir Henry to walk **alone** across the moor at night?

1. Stapleton looks like Sir Hugo who must be his ancestor too.

2. Stapleton wants Sir Henry to disappear so that he could inherit Baskerville Hall.

3. False, Holmes thinks that Stapleton will invite Sir Henry to dinner.

4. False, he will do everything without question.

17

1. True, so he doesn't notice that they don't take the train to London.

2. Lestrade, a very clever detective from Scotland Yard.

3. False, Beryl is not there.

4. True, so we can imagine that the detectives will take care of him when he is on the moor.

What is the trick?

Holmes' **plan** is simple: Stapleton must **think** that Sir Henry is alone at Baskerville Hall. In this way Stapleton will not fear Holmes can **intervene** to defend his friend. Holmes is playing a **trick** on Stapleton to **catch** him with Lestrade's **help**.

18

1. The detectives can hardly see in the distance because it is foggy.

2. Because Sir Henry is in great danger.

3. He turns round and is horrified to see the hound after him.

4. Suddenly an enormous and dreadful hound is running after Sir Henry. Holmes and Watson shoot at the beast but they only hurt it, it howls horribly but it still runs and jumps on its victim.

19

1. He fainted and fell on the ground unconscious.

2. Because Stapleton put something glowing on his dog.

3. Now that the hound is dead and Sir Henry is safe, the three detectives go to find Stapleton but he is not at home. Instead they find Beryl locked in a room and tied up to a post because she disagreed with her husband.

4. True, the detectives can't find him at home.

5. We know that Beryl doesn't share her husband's opinion about Sir Henry because she sighs with relief when she learns that Sir Henry is not dead.

20

Why did Stapleton go to Grimpen Mire?

After the dinner with Sir Henry, Stapleton heard the shots and decided to escape; he went to Grimpen Mire but it was foggy and too dark to see, so Holmes explains that he got stuck into the mire and probably died there.

1. On a small island in Grimpen Mire.

2. Yes, she shows them the place where he kept his dog.

3. Holmes notices Sir Henry's missing boot, Stapleton used it for Sir Henry's smell.

4. He needs to rest and get away from Baskerville Hall.

4e
Read in English
MACBETH
D'après
William
Shakespeare
Version audio à télécharger
HARRAP'S SCHOOL
Réalisé avec des enseignants

3e
Read in English
Doctor
Faustus
D'après Christopher
Marlowe
Version audio à télécharger
HARRAP'S SCHOOL
Réalisé avec des enseignants

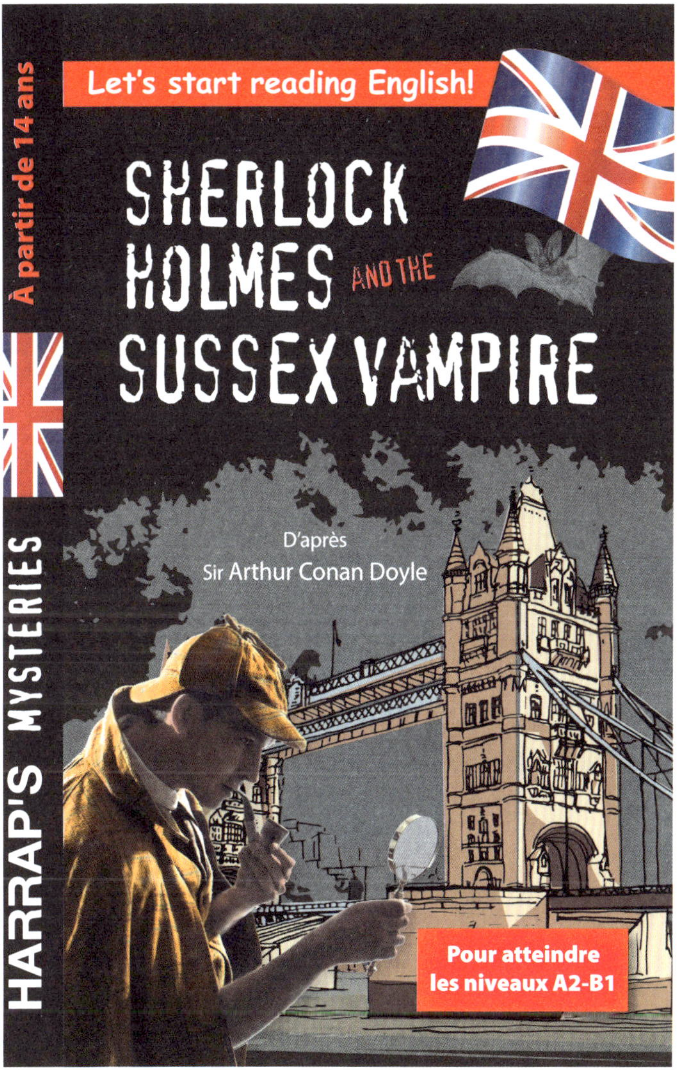
Let's start reading English!
À partir de 14 ans
SHERLOCK
HOLMES
AND THE
SUSSEX VAMPIRE
D'après
Sir Arthur Conan Doyle
HARRAP'S MYSTERIES
Pour atteindre
les niveaux A2-B1

CRÉDITS PHOTOGRAPHIQUES
© shutterstock.com - © thegraphicsfairy.com

PAPIER À BASE DE FIBRES CERTIFIÉES
HARRAP s'engage pour l'environnement en réduisant l'empreinte carbone de ses livres. Celle de cet exemplaire est de :
600 g éq. CO_2
Rendez-vous sur www.larousse-durable.fr

Imprimé en Roumanie chez Canale
Dépôt légal : mars 2020 – 325365/01
N° de projet : 11043071 – mars 2020